皮皮與波西

♥IREAD

皮皮與波西：聖誕樹

繪　　　圖	阿克賽爾・薛弗勒
譯　　　者	酪梨壽司
責任編輯	郭心蘭
美術編輯	郭雅萍

發 行 人	劉振強
出 版 者	三民書局股份有限公司
地　　　址	臺北市復興北路 386 號 (復北門市)
	臺北市重慶南路一段 61 號 (重南門市)
電　　　話	(02)25006600
網　　　址	三民網路書店 https://www.sanmin.com.tw

出版日期	初版一刷 2019 年 1 月
	初版三刷 2022 年 3 月
書籍編號	S858610
I S B N	978-957-14-6537-1

Originally published in the English language as PIP AND POSY:
THE CHRISTMAS TREE
Text Copyright © Nosy Crow Ltd 2018
Illustration Copyright © Axel Scheffler 2018
Copyright licensed by Nosy Crow Ltd.
Chinese translation right © 2018 San Min Book Co., Ltd.

小山丘官網

皮皮與波西

聖誕樹

阿克賽爾‧薛弗勒／圖　酪梨壽司／譯

小山丘

聖誕節快到了，皮皮和波西一起
去挑了一棵聖誕樹。

到家後，他們把樹種在花盆裡。

接著烤了餅乾，準備掛在聖誕樹上。

五ㄨˇ片ㄆㄧㄢˋ餅ㄅㄧㄥˇ乾ㄍㄢ看ㄎㄢˋ起ㄑㄧˇ來ㄌㄞˊ真ㄓㄣ漂ㄆㄧㄠˋ亮ㄌㄧㄤˋ。

波ㄅㄛ西ㄒㄧ去ㄑㄩˋ拿ㄋㄚˊ四ㄙˋ根ㄍㄣ拐ㄍㄨㄞˇ杖ㄓㄤˋ糖ㄊㄤˊ。

但_{ㄉㄢˋ}當_{ㄉㄤ}她_{ㄊㄚ}回_{ㄏㄨㄟˊ}來_{ㄌㄞˊ}時_{ㄕˊ}，
有_{ㄧㄡˇ}一_ㄧ片_{ㄆㄧㄢˋ}餅_{ㄅㄧㄥˇ}乾_{ㄍㄢ}不_{ㄅㄨˋ}見_{ㄐㄧㄢˋ}了_{ㄌㄜ˙}。

「真_{ㄓㄣ}奇_{ㄑㄧˊ}怪_{ㄍㄨㄞˋ}，」她_{ㄊㄚ}說_{ㄕㄨㄛ}。 「原_{ㄩㄢˊ}本_{ㄅㄣˇ}有_{ㄧㄡˇ}五_{ㄨˇ}片_{ㄆㄧㄢˋ}
餅_{ㄅㄧㄥˇ}乾_{ㄍㄢ}，現_{ㄒㄧㄢˋ}在_{ㄗㄞˋ}只_{ㄓˇ}剩_{ㄕㄥˋ}下_{ㄒㄧㄚˋ}四_{ㄙˋ}片_{ㄆㄧㄢˋ}。」

皮皮將拐杖糖掛上聖誕樹時，
波西去找巧克力鈴鐺。

但當波西回來時，她注意到
有一根拐杖糖不見了。

「原本有四根拐杖糖，」她說。

「但現在只剩下三根。」

波（ㄅㄛ）西（ㄒㄧ）去（ㄑㄩ）拿（ㄋㄚ）聖（ㄕㄥ）誕（ㄉㄢ）星（ㄒㄧㄥ）星（ㄒㄧㄥ）。

皮（ㄆㄧ）皮（ㄆㄧ）將（ㄐㄧㄤ）巧（ㄑㄧㄠ）克（ㄎㄜ）力（ㄌㄧ）鈴（ㄌㄧㄥ）鐺（ㄉㄤ）掛（ㄍㄨㄚ）上（ㄕㄤ）聖（ㄕㄥ）誕（ㄉㄢ）樹（ㄕㄨ）。

但當波西回來時，她發現所有的裝飾品通通都不見了！

喔，天啊！

接著波西發現皮皮躺在沙發上。

「你還好嗎，皮皮？」
波西問。

「不好，」皮皮說。

「我覺得不太舒服。」

可憐的皮皮！

波西幫皮皮倒了
一杯水。

「對不起，波西，」
皮皮說。
「我把所有的
裝飾品都吃光了。」

「是啊，我知道。」
波西說。

他們決定出門呼吸新鮮空氣。

皮皮很快就覺得好一點了。

當他們回到屋子裡，
看到了空空的聖誕樹。

「我們要不要用紙來做
一些裝飾品?」皮皮問。

「真是個超棒的主意，皮皮！」波西說。

於是他們做了紙鏈、星星和愛心。

聖（ㄕㄥˋ）誕（ㄉㄢˋ）樹（ㄕㄨˋ）看（ㄎㄢˋ）起（ㄑㄧˇ）來（ㄌㄞˊ）漂（ㄆㄧㄠˋ）亮（ㄌㄧㄤˋ）極（ㄐㄧˊ）了（ㄌㄜ˙）。

隔天一大早，皮皮和波西發現了聖誕樹下的禮物。

他們決定從小包的開始拆。

波西的禮物是一把超棒的
點點圖案剪刀。而皮皮的則是……

一枝可愛的
彩虹圖案牙刷！

「這正是我想要的！」皮皮說。
太棒啦！

聖誕快樂，
皮皮和波西！

It was Christmas time and Pip and Posy
went to fetch a Christmas tree.

When they got home,
they put the tree in a pot.

Then they baked biscuits to hang on it.

The five biscuits looked really pretty.

Posy went to get four candy canes.

But when she came back,
one of the biscuits was missing.

"That's odd," she said. "There were five
biscuits, but now there are only four."

Posy went to find the chocolate bells
while Pip put the candy canes on the tree.

But when Posy came back she noticed
that one of the candy canes was missing.

"There were four candy canes," she said.
"But now there are only three."

Posy went to get the Christmas star.

But when Posy came back she saw that all the decorations had **completely disappeared!**

Pip put the chocolate bells on the tree.

Oh dear!

Then Posy noticed that Pip was lying on the sofa.

"Are you ok, Pip?" said Posy.

"No," said Pip.

"I feel sick."

Poor Pip!

Posy brought Pip
a glass of water.

"I'm sorry, Posy,"
said Pip.
"I ate ALL the
decorations."

"Yes, I know,"
said Posy.

They decided to go outside for some fresh air.   Pip soon felt a bit better.

When they came back in,
the tree looked rather bare.

"Shall we make some paper
decorations now?" said Pip.

"That's a VERY good idea, Pip,"
said Posy.

So they made paperchains,
and stars and hearts.

And the tree looked beautiful.

Early next morning, Pip and Posy found
presents under the Christmas tree.

They decided to open the little ones first.

a lovely rainbow toothbrush!

Posy's present was a nice, new pair of spotty scissors. And Pip's was . . .

"That's **just** what I need," said Pip.

Hooray!

Happy Christmas,
Pip and Posy!

繪者簡介

阿克賽爾・薛弗勒　Axel Scheffler

1957年出生於德國漢堡市，25歲時前往英國就讀巴斯藝術學院。他的插畫風格幽默又不失優雅，最著名的當屬《古飛樂》(Gruffalo) 系列作品，不僅榮獲英國多項繪本大獎，譯作超過40種語言，還曾改編為動畫，深受全球觀眾喜愛，是世界知名的繪本作家。薛弗勒現居英國，持續創作中。

譯者簡介

酪梨壽司

當過記者、玩過行銷，在紐約和東京流浪多年後，終於返鄉定居的臺灣媽媽。出沒於臉書專頁「酪梨壽司」與個人部落格「酪梨壽司的日記」。